Material Drug Dreams

MATERIAL DRUG DREAMS

First edition. April 8, 2025.

Written by K.M.DRAYVEN.

Chapter One

The Season That Never Fall Again

LONDON, 1993

London, in the year 1993, stood at a peculiar crossroads—

An empire's capital that no longer ruled, yet still commanded reverence in its every breath.

The River Thames moved with ancient indifference, its waters thick with memory, whispering the long-forgotten prayers of monarchs, martyrs, and mercenaries. Fog rolled in from the riverbanks at dawn, cloaking the city in the same grey veil worn since the days of Victoria

—mourning, perhaps, something long buried but not quite dead.

The air was touched by coal and cold stone. Buildings stood shoulder to shoulder like sentinels—Victorian red-brick terraces, soot-kissed Gothic chapels, and Georgian façades faded but proud. The skyline, though stirring, had not yet surrendered entirely to steel and glass. St. Paul's still held dominion, and the Houses of Parliament cast their spired ilhouettes across the city like watchful elders.

The public still relied on red telephone boxes, and black cabs reigned preme in the streets. Men in three-piece suits passed punks in leather ets, each side barely acknowledging the other.

he old and new Britain walked the same pavements, but seldom —and sometimes, if you watched long enough, shadows between noved when no one walked at all.

In Westminster, the mood remained austere. The government, now post-Thatcher, wore its authority like a stiff collar—orderly, if uncertain. There was murmuring in Parliament, grumblings in the press, and the quiet resilience of a people who had endured war, rationing, and recession. Yet, in the corners of Whitehall, lights flickered when they shouldn't, and files were occasionally found altered—by no hand that could be traced.

Music seeped from pubs in Soho and jazz clubs in Southwark. In the East End, whispers of development stirred unease amongst families who had lived there for generations. And though the city was weary of change, it could not escape the pull of progress—nor outrun the past that walked just one step behind it.

But beneath the car horns, beneath the clatter of the Underground and the shouts of newsboys, something else lingered.

London was old—not just in age, but in soul.

And old cities have long memories.

Some say she never forgets.

Others say she watches.

And a rare few, those who still remember the names scratched into the underside of crypt doors and clocktower beams, say she hungers.

AND IF LONDON TRULY watched—

then her gaze often fell, uneasy and unblinking,

upon a forgotten northern rise where the fog refused to lift,

and where Aetherford Silver University stood like an unanswered question etched in limestone and silence.

Aetherford Silver University was not merely a place of learning—it was a citadel of remembrance.

Founded in 1489, during the reign of Henry VII, its limestone arches had seen the march of redcoats, the hush of candlelit treaties, and the ink-blotted secrets of men who wrote history in footnotes and blood.

Located on the city's secluded northern edge—where the fog lingered longer, and time walked slower—Aetherford was an institution shrouded in prestige and whispered myth.

It was said the library's restricted wing held texts too dangerous for daylight, and that the bell in the South Tower rang once, long ago, at an hour no clock dared count.

Alumni included lords, spies, authors, and at least three unsolved disappearances. Professors dressed in robes heavy with tradition; students in tweed and ambition. Latin mottos were engraved into every stone lintel, though few remembered their true meaning. Fewer still dared translate the inscription above the Hall of Spheres.

And yet, despite its air of timelessness, something had changed.

The wind no longer hummed the same.

The ivy on the East Wing had begun to wither.

And some students swore that shadows lingered too long beneath the arches after dusk.

It was here—at the very centre of legacy's pulse—that the silence was broken.

No one remembered autumn that year.

As though the leaves had struck a quiet pact with the branches—to never fall again.

But something else descended from the skies that morning.

Something far more unsettling.

The clouds parted with regal reluctance, like curtains drawn back before an unwelcome performance, as a jet-black Merlin Blackhawk carved a path through the London sky. It came down not upon a helipad, nor any sterile stretch of tarmac—but upon the lawn of Aetherford Silver University, where legacy dressed itself in marble, and ambition walked in polished leather and tailored tweed.

Its rotors sliced the silence with sovereign precision.

Below, students scattered like startled starlings, their notebooks raised against the downwash, their conversations sheared in half. Some stood frozen, eyes wide—not in fear of the machine, but in awe of the presence it carried.

Because it wasn't the noise.

It wasn't even the aircraft.

It was him.

The side door drifted open mid-air, as though reluctant to part from the world it came from.

And then he stepped out—unhurried, unaffected.

Geltorn Brith Earl.

A name spoken like an incantation in certain corridors of power, and barely whispered in others. A silhouette sculpted in tailored charcoal wool, his gloved hands at ease, his eyes veiled behind softly smoked lenses that caught the morning light like secrets withheld. One hand adjusted a silver timepiece that had outlived wars; the other slipped into the pocket of a coat cut like it belonged to a dynasty.

When his shoes met the lawn, it wasn't a landing.

It was a return.

As if the very ground had once known him—and now remembered.

He did not arrive at the university.

He claimed it.

As though he had etched the blueprints of its great halls in some forgotten century,

and returned now only to resume what had once been interrupted. But not every moment in London wore a cloak of shadows.

THAT AFTERNOON, AS the autumn sun dared to peek through the clouds—golden and defiant—Aetherford Silver's campus stirred with something dangerously close to joy. The buzz of gossip raced faster than the library clock's hands, and in tucked-away courtyards, students laughed nervously, unsure whether they'd witnessed a scandal, a legend, or simply a man with better taste than the Chancellor himself.

Geltorn Brith Earl strolled through the old stone arches like a memory that never aged.

Girls whispered his name like it was a forbidden novel title.

Boys watched him with equal parts admiration and suspicion.

By the fountain near the Hall of Spheres, where ivy curled like question marks along the walls, a curious trio finally gathered the courage to approach him—two in cardigans, one with a camera still swinging from his neck.

"Are you... Are you a visiting professor?" the boldest asked, with a nervous grin.

Geltorn paused. Turned. His expression unreadable—but not unkind.

A silence lingered just long enough to make them regret asking.

Then, finally, he spoke.

"Something like that," he said, voice smooth as aged scotch and twice as dangerous.

"Let's call it... an elective in reality."

And just like that, he walked on—leaving behind a trail of cologne, confusion, and the faintest trace of a smirk.

But before the shadows could reclaim the moment, a voice pierced the silence—

"Nice entrance, mystery man."

The speaker stood at the base of the stone steps—arms crossed, one brow arched like a punctuation mark at the end of a question no one dared ask.

Her name was Valeska Monroe.

Daughter of a foreign diplomat and an expelled art historian, she was the kind of woman who wore secrets like perfume—faint, expensive, and impossible to ignore. Her scarf was vintage Hermès, her boots military-grade. No one knew what she studied at Aetherford, or if she studied at all. But her file in the admissions office had a corner burned off, and every professor knew better than to ask her to submit anything on time.

Next to her, hunched over a sketchbook with ink-stained fingers and an absentminded smile, sat Theo Grimsley—the youngest student ever accepted into the university's covert Department of Temporal Ethics. Theo saw the world in graphs and ghosts. He claimed he once mapped a dream. People laughed. The next day, two students found themselves walking in their sleep... straight into the Thames.

And trailing behind them both, fidgeting with a pocket radio older than he was, came Declan Veer. A scholarship boy from East London with a photographic memory and a knack for locking himself inside forbidden archives. Declan wasn't particularly brave. But he knew things. Things no one should.

They watched Geltorn Brith Earl with the same fascination one reserves for a lion let loose in a ballroom.

Valeska tilted her head. "You must be the one they warned us about."

Geltorn adjusted his silver timepiece without looking at her.

"Then they warned you too late."

Declan let out a low whistle. "He talks like he's in a Cold War film. I kinda like it."

Theo didn't look up from his sketchbook. "His aura just cracked my ink. That's not supposed to happen."

"His aura?" Valeska muttered. "Darling, we haven't even verified if he has a pulse."

Geltorn took one slow step toward them, shoes silent on the old stone. "I have more than a pulse, Miss Monroe. I have a memory."

Valeska's smirk faltered—just a flicker.

And that's when it happened.

Behind them, the wind shifted.

A sudden gust spiraled through the cloister, and the rusted letterbox beneath the ivy groaned open as if woken from a long slumber.

Declan turned first. "What the hell?"

Valeska approached it cautiously. "That box hasn't opened since—"

Theo interrupted, "—since 1953, after the Incident. And only once before that, in 1882. It's not supposed to open. It's... curated."

Inside the letterbox sat a single envelope.

Black wax. No seal.

Just a name, written in ink that shimmered ever so slightly—like it hadn't decided what colour to settle on.

KAI STARLING.

They all fell quiet.

Geltorn finally turned toward it, his eyes unreadable behind the smoked lenses.

"Looks like the game's already begun."

Theo picked up the envelope, his fingers trembling slightly. "There's a card inside..."

He opened it.

A single line, handwritten:

"Your silence was never protection."

And beneath that, the faintest watermark—almost invisible unless you tilted the paper just right:

A detective's calling card. Signed: K.S.

Valeska whispered, "Kai Starling... wasn't he the one who solved the Lazarus Gallery disappearances?"

Declan frowned. "No. They say he solved it. But no one ever found the files."

Theo blinked. "Because someone erased them."

The bell in the South Tower rang again—twice this time.

And from somewhere deep beneath the university, behind the locked vaults and wards that even Theo dared not map, something turned in its sleep.

Later that night, when the campus quieted and the echoes in the cloisters had faded, Geltorn Brith Earl sat alone beneath the cracked skylight of his quarters in the West Wing—a room that had once belonged to a 17th-century alchemist who vanished without a trace.

On the desk before him:

A polished mahogany box, inlaid with a sigil no living student could decipher—though the ghost of a professor once claimed it only appeared under moonlight.

He opened it with reverent precision.

Inside were six vials, nestled like relics from a forgotten cathedral.

Each bore a name forbidden in lecture halls but murmured in shadows:

Mythrex – the memory thief.

Zephyra – the dream wanderer.

Obelix – the mind sharpened to a blade.

Solivane – light in liquid form.

Umbrosin – the whisper between truths.

Erosyn – pleasure so divine, it kills.

HE IGNORED FIVE.

His fingers hovered over Mythrex—half-empty, labeled only with a number: 0.3.

He rolled up his sleeve.

Silver veins shimmered beneath his skin—no longer human, not entirely. The drug hadn't just passed through him. It had written itself into his blood.

He injected the dose like a man sipping tea before bed. No drama.

And the change came instantly.

His pupils expanded until the candlelight was swallowed whole. His lungs slowed.

The world... fractured.

Visions rushed through the seams of reality:

—A burning city with no sky.

—A woman screaming with a key carved into her spine.

—A chessboard laid out in a cathedral whose altar was time itself.

—A tower of glass falling into an ocean of teeth.

—And his own name... spoken by someone he had never met but somehow loved.

His hand gripped the desk as a low hum vibrated through his bones.

This wasn't hallucination.

This was prophecy.

Mythrex was banned in 147 nations. Said to unlock the "Third Record"—a timeline not yet lived, but already woven into the marrow of fate.

Few survived it. Fewer still came back sane.

Only one had ever adapted to it.

Geltorn Brith Earl.

As the drug rippled through his nervous system like liquid fate, he whispered into the empty room—

"Show me what I've forgotten."

And somewhere in the library's restricted wing, a book slammed shut—no hands, no wind, no cause.

The flame of a single candle flared blue... then went out.

THE ROOM EXHALED A strange stillness, like the very air was waiting.

A knock.

It wasn't loud.

It didn't need to be.

Just three deliberate strikes, steady as a metronome counting down something inevitable.

Geltorn tilted his head, movements slower now, the drug coiling in his bloodstream like smoke in a sealed jar.

He rose, every joint stiff with aftershock, and approached the door with the calm of a man who's already seen how the story ends.

One step.

Another.

Then—his vision fractured. Not blurred—shattered.

Like light through broken stained glass.

His body crumpled.

No warning. No cry. Just silence, and then the dull thud of him hitting the cold stone floor.

The candle on the desk flickered violently, then died—smoke curling into a question mark.

The door opened.

But no one stepped through.

Only the scent of winter and something metallic, like old coins or blood long dried.

From the corridor outside, a voice floated in—

"Still too early, Geltorn. But you're remembering."

And beneath the floorboards, something began to tick.

Slow.

Deliberate.

Alive.

Geltorn woke gasping.

But the air tasted wrong.

Too sweet.

Too still.

Like the breath of a room that had been sealed shut for centuries.

He was no longer in his quarters.

The cracked skylight was gone.

The stone floor beneath him had turned to polished obsidian—cold and gleaming, like the inside of a coffin carved from shadow.

Above him, symbols danced across the ceiling in silent flame—languages he didn't know, but somehow understood.

A voice echoed—not from the walls, but from inside his mind.

"Welcome back, Archivist."

He tried to move, but his limbs were heavy, like soaked cloth.

His veins itched where the Mythrex had entered.

And then—he saw it.

A figure, cloaked in smoke, seated in a high-backed chair that hadn't been there a second ago.

Its face was obscured. Not by shadow. But by possibility—as if it wore every face he'd ever seen, and none of them at once.

"You weren't supposed to remember so soon," it whispered.

"But the timeline is fraying. They're watching. He's watching."

Geltorn tried to speak, but his voice failed him.

The figure stood, one hand outstretched.

"You've opened the Third Record. Now you must find the others."

IT HANDED HIM SOMETHING.

A compass. But its needle didn't point north.

It spun wildly before slowing... toward Kai Starling's name, etched faintly across its glass.

And then—

Bang.

He snapped upright in bed, breath ragged, sweat soaking the sheets.

He was back in his room.

The skylight cracked.

The mahogany box still open.

Only...

One more vial was missing.

Erosyn.

And carved into the desk, in a handwriting that wasn't his—

"Find the girl with the key."

A knock hit the door—this time, loud.

Not from this dream, but the waking world.

Kai's voice echoed faintly—"Geltorn!"

The figure tilted its head.

"Your anchor," it said. "Hold fast."

It stepped backward into the shifting door—and was gone.

The room collapsed in silence.

And that's when Valeska appeared—though she didn't walk in. She fell through the flame-written ceiling, landing hard beside Geltorn.

Her scarf caught fire the instant she touched the floor, but she didn't scream.

Instead, she looked at him—eyes wild, furious.

"You bastard," she spat. "You pulled me into your trip?"

Geltorn stared, stunned.

"You're not supposed to be here," he muttered.

Valeska smirked, brushing soot from her coat. "Neither are you."

And then, just as quickly—the world tore in two.

AND THEN, JUST AS QUICKLY—THE world tore in two.

Everything inverted.

Like falling up.

Like breathing backward.

Like time exhaling.

Geltorn woke, gasping.

The room was dim. The cracked skylight above offered no stars, only the dull ache of dawn pressing through fog.

But the air—still wrong.

Still sweet.

Still sealed.

His sheets were soaked in sweat. His pulse stammered.

He wasn't alone.

At the foot of his bed, Kai Starling stood, eyes wide behind wire-rimmed glasses, one hand still hovering near the door handle.

"Jesus, Geltorn. I've been banging on your door for ten minutes. You sounded like you were—" He stopped.

The mahogany box.

Open.

The vials visible.

Kai's gaze locked onto them.

His brow furrowed. "Is that...?"

"Don't," Geltorn croaked. "Don't say it."

Kai stepped forward. "You're bleeding."

Geltorn looked down. A trickle of silver leaked from the inside of his left arm—not blood, not quite. Not anymore.

"I didn't mean to go that deep," he murmured.

Kai knelt beside the bed. "You took Mythrex again? Are you out of your mind?"

"I had to."

"You don't have to do anything that burns your brain from the inside out." He grabbed a cloth, trying to wipe the metallic sheen from Geltorn's skin. It didn't work. "It's binding to your nerves now. You're not using it—it's using you."

The desk.

Geltorn turned, almost afraid.

The message was still there.

Find the girl with the key.

Kai followed his gaze. "What the hell is that?"

"I didn't write it."

"Then who did?"

"I don't know."

Kai stepped back like the room was suddenly radioactive.

And then—

A scent.

Sweet. Cloying.

Unmistakable.

Kai's eyes snapped to the box again.

"Wait. Is Erosyn missing?"

Geltorn didn't answer.

Kai's voice dropped. "Who did you bring with you?"

The silence answered for him.

Valeska.

Somewhere else in Aetherford, a girl woke in a sweat, her hands glowing faintly beneath the skin.

She remembered obsidian.

She remembered fire.

She remembered Geltorn's voice saying her name like a curse and a prayer.

Back in the West Wing, Geltorn finally met Kai's eyes.

"She's in it now," he said.

Kai paled.

"You didn't just take the drug," he said. "You opened the Record."

Geltorn nodded slowly. "And now we're all inside it."

Ash & Amber

The storm outside had softened into a steady drizzle, tapping against the stained-glass windows of Professor Alaric Thorne's study like a polite intruder.

Inside, the room was thick with age and thought—books lining the walls floor to ceiling, some still humming faintly from past enchantments. The fire snapped lazily in the hearth. The air smelled of ash, leather, and old promises.

Kai Starling sat across from the professor in a high-backed chair that had likely held more secrets than students. One leg crossed neatly over the other, a glass of amber brandy resting untouched in his hand, its warmth seeping into his skin.

He hadn't taken a sip.

Not yet.

Professor Thorne, red-bearded and sunken-eyed from decades of sleepless scholarship, sipped his own drink with visible weariness. "You have your mother's stillness," he murmured. "And Geltorn's eyes."

Kai tilted his head slightly, curious. "So you believe it, then?"

"I do," Thorne said, voice like old velvet. "I was there when your name was entered in the ledger. Starling by choice. Earl by blood."

Kai finally took a small sip of the brandy, letting it burn slowly down his throat. "He doesn't know."

"Not fully. Not yet," Thorne said. "But he will. You're not here by accident."

Kai leaned forward slightly, his tone light, but his eyes gleaming. "I've never believed in accidents. I believe in proximity. Pressure. Leverage."

The professor gave a short chuckle. "That's why I agreed to this meeting. You remind me of Geltorn before the drugs. Before the voices started. Cold on the outside. But burning to understand."

Kai let the silence settle for a moment before breaking it with a scalpel-sharp question.

"You've seen the Third Record, haven't you?"

Thorne stiffened just a touch. A flicker. Barely there—but Kai caught it.

"I was younger," the professor said. "Foolish. Thought I could decode fate like an equation. Mythrex nearly shattered my mind."

"But you came back," Kai pressed.

"Barely. I came back... different."

Kai's gaze sharpened. "Then you know what he's becoming."

Thorne looked away. "Yes."

"And you're still letting him walk this path?"

The professor sighed. "Because we can't stop it now. We can only guide it. Or... bear witness."

Kai stood, slowly. He walked toward the window, brandy swirling in his glass like amber prophecy.

He spoke without turning. "You think I'm his shadow."

"I think you're his mirror," Thorne said quietly.

Kai smiled. "No. I'm his counterweight."

Thunder murmured in the distance. Kai set his untouched glass down gently on the table.

"When the Record opens fully," he said, "someone has to hold the line."

He stepped into the firelight, casting a long silhouette against the old stones.

"I intend to be ready."

The fire behind him faded as Kai stepped into the corridor, the echo of his footsteps muffled by thick maroon carpet and thicker secrets. Somewhere deeper in the ancient ribs of Aetherford Silver University, a bell tolled twice. Not for the hour—no, this bell was ceremonial. Rare. A signal known only to certain circles.

Someone had died.

He reached the upper landing just as the cold rushed in—a gust of night air seeping through a half-cracked window. Below, students gathered near the west courtyard, voices hushed and brittle.

Kai didn't descend.

Instead, he turned toward the east wing.

Toward the library.

The Letter

In the quietest corner of the library—where only the desperate or the damned dared read past midnight—Kai spotted the shift. A book, dislodged. A slip of paper peeking out like a tongue behind teeth.

He pulled it free.

Not an envelope.

A folded parchment, off-white and whisper-thin, smelled faintly of cinnamon and burnt wax.

Just two words, handwritten in an angular script:

Look deeper.

Tucked inside was a photo.

A moment frozen in time: six students, arms linked. Geltorn in the center.

The girl beside him—yes, Kai recognised her.

Ione Blackbriar.

Dead. Less than an hour ago.

But something was wrong with the image.

The sixth figure in the back... hadn't been there before.

Kai. Staring directly at the lens.

But the photo was dated 1984.

THE NIGHT BREAKS

Back in the courtyard, the whispers became screams.

Kai returned to the hall just as the doors burst open. Rain trailed in behind three students—one of them sobbing.

"It's Ione," someone gasped. "Observatory. She's not—she's—"

He didn't wait.

The Body

Ione lay beneath the great dome of the observatory. No blood. No bruises. Just a stillness that didn't belong to the living—or the dead.

Her eyes were open.

Not in terror.

In recognition.

Above her, the glass ceiling shimmered with a strange frost. Etched in the condensation was a symbol that hadn't been seen in the world since the fall of Mythrex:

A sigil shaped like a closed eye inside an hourglass.

Time withheld.

BY THE TIME THE CONSTABLES were summoned, the symbol had faded. The body remained untouched.

Kai stood alone at the edge of the room, holding the photo in one hand and the letter in the other.

He whispered, "The past is bleeding through."

Outside, the drizzle ceased.

And on the far side of the quad, the only red maple on campus still refused to shed a single leaf—its fire frozen in defiance.

In London, 1993, the seasons changed like politics—quick, sharp, and merciless.
But once, there was a year where one tree didn't bow.
A season that stayed too long.
A memory that wouldn't fall.
Some say it was grief.
Others, a spell.
But Kai Starling would come to learn the truth—
That sometimes, time refuses to move...
...because it's waiting for someone to set it right.

"The Season That Never Fell Again" is not just about a stubborn tree or a lost life.

It is about a moment in time—frozen by pain, grief, or forbidden magic—that refuses to fade.

It asks: What if a season could mourn?

What if memory itself could hold its breath, waiting for the right hands to undo what was broken? "

Chapter Two

The Light Beneath the Floorboards

The morning after felt like a silence no one had earned.

Aetherford Silver University stood unchanged on the outside—its towers draped in mist, its lawns slick with rain—but something beneath the stone was different. It wasn't just the weather. It was as if the building itself had held its breath.

Kai Starling stood in the long corridor of Westgrove Hall, coat buttoned, gloves on. His expression was still, unreadable, but his mind was moving like a sharpened pendulum.

Behind him, Valeska Monroe walked at a short distance, arms crossed, scarf coiled tight around her throat like a red warning.

"You felt it too," she said softly.

Kai didn't turn. "The dream wasn't just mine. You were pulled into it. That doesn't happen by chance."

"I don't dream," she muttered. "Not unless someone else is dreaming loud enough to drag me in."

They stopped before an old wooden door. Room 213. Geltorn's quarters.

A moment later, it opened.

Geltorn stood barefoot, shirt half-buttoned, eyes ringed with the weight of something unslept. But his voice was calm.

"I knew you'd come."

Kai walked in without a word. Valeska followed.

The room was dim, papers scattered across the desk like a broken map. A compass sat in the center—still twitching, its needle quivering without direction.

Valeska pointed. “It hasn’t stopped since last night.”

Geltorn stared at it, jaw tense. “It points at nothing. It’s spinning like it’s afraid.”

Kai picked it up gently, then placed it into his coat pocket.

“It’s not pointing at nothing,” he said. “It’s pointing at something that doesn’t want to be found.”

Before anyone could respond, a knock came at the door.

Professor Thorne.

But he wasn’t alone.

Behind him stood Theo Grimsley, the boy genius from Temporal Ethics—his hair in disarray, shirt ink-stained, fingers twitching with barely-contained knowledge.

And beside him—Declan Veer, silent, observant, eyes always scanning, like he’d memorized the shadows in the corridor.

Thorne looked grim. “There’s been... a discovery.”

No one moved.

Then Theo spoke, voice shaking slightly.

“In the east wing. Basement floor. Beneath the archives.”

Valeska narrowed her eyes. “What kind of discovery?”

Declan answered for him, voice low. “A body.”

Kai’s heart didn’t skip. It slowed.

Geltorn’s eyes flared. “Who?”

Thorne’s voice was a whisper now.

“We don’t know. Not yet. But the place was sealed off in 1974. No one’s been down there in decades.”

Kai nodded once, then turned.

“Show me.”

The lower levels of Aetherford were unlike the rest of the university—colder, untouched, and half-forgotten. The stairs spiraled down behind a locked iron gate Thorne had opened with a brass key shaped like a question mark.

Kai descended first, his boots silent on the stone.

The air changed with every step. Dust turned metallic. Cold gave way to something...older. It didn't smell like rot. It smelled like waiting.

Theo flicked on a dim lantern. "They used to store artifacts here. Objects too unstable or... politically dangerous to be studied in public."

Valeska whispered, "Then why was it sealed?"

Thorne didn't answer.

The corridor ended at a door of thick wood, blackened with age. Its hinges were iron. The keyhole had been filled with wax decades ago.

But the door was already slightly open.

That was the first wrong thing.

Kai noticed the indentation on the floorboards just beneath the door a faint groove, like someone had forced it open with a blade thin enough to slip past time itself.

He pushed the door wider.

Inside: darkness, then lantern light.

A single room. Stone walls. Floorboards warped by damp.

And in the center—a shape.

Covered in a decayed university cloak. The deep navy fabric still clung to the form beneath like a second skin.

Not a skeleton.

Fresh.

Valeska exhaled sharply. "This... this isn't from the '70s."

Kai said nothing. He stepped forward, slow and deliberate. The others hung back.

He crouched beside the body, studying everything—not just the obvious.

The way the hand was clenched.

The torn hem near the ankle.

The faint chalk mark on the wall—half-erased, like someone had tried to wipe it away.

Then he saw it.

Beneath the floorboard beside the body, the faintest sliver of light.

He pulled off his glove, touched the edge.

Warm.

He looked up. "Someone tried to hide something down here. Something that leaks heat... and time."

Declan stepped closer. "How could it still be warm?"

Kai's voice was calm. "Because it's not part of this world anymore."

He stood, brushed dust from his coat, and turned to Theo.

"Get me the archives from the restricted Mythrex lectures. Every page that was redacted after 1981."

Theo blinked. "That'll take hours."

Kai's eyes sharpened.

"You have two."

Valeska turned to Thorne. "Do you think it's connected to the dream we shared?"

The professor was pale now. "More than that. I think the dream was a warning."

Kai was already moving toward the far wall. "It wasn't a warning."

He touched the chalk sigil again.

"It was a call."

Then he pressed two fingers against the wall.

Click.

The stone behind the body shifted. Not a door. A panel.

A second room, smaller—round, lined with mirrors that had no reflections.

And on a pedestal in the center...

...a pendulum, swinging.

But there was no mechanism. No ceiling string. It hung in air—swinging.

Back and forth.

Back and forth.

Tick.

Tock.

Not seconds.

Names.

Kai stepped in. Every swing whispered a word only he could hear. Names from his blood. From his forgotten memories.

He smiled, faintly.

"Time's not broken," he whispered.

"It's been rewritten."

Kai stared at the pendulum. It swung not with time, but with memory. With blood.

He stepped closer. The names whispered weren't just from his past.

They were his.

Fragments of lives he'd never lived—at least not in this body. Places he'd never seen but somehow remembered. Fires. Cities that no longer existed. A girl with silver eyes who said his name before he ever knew it.

Behind him, Theo murmured, "This isn't just a relic."

Kai nodded. "It's an anchor."

Declan tilted his head. "To what?"

Kai turned toward them. His face was calm, but the air around him felt stretched, like reality was being held together by thread.

"The dream wasn't prophecy. It was recall. A memory buried so deep, it could only speak through sleep."

Valeska stepped beside him. "Whose memory?"

Kai looked at her—then at the pendulum. "Ours."

She went still.

Theo blinked rapidly. "You're saying... we've all been here before?"

"No," Kai replied. "We never left."

A silence fell over the room, thick and grave.

Professor Thorne swallowed hard. "This place was built over something. Long before the university. Long before London."

Theo's lantern flickered.

Valeska crossed her arms, voice low. "What was down here?"

Thorne looked at her, then at Kai. "A machine."

Kai corrected him. "A ritual."

Declan stepped toward the mirrored walls. "But what does it do?"

Kai looked at the pendulum again.

"It dreams."

Valeska frowned. "Dreams what?"

Kai's voice dropped to a whisper.

"Us."

The pendulum swung—no wind, no string, no mercy.

Declan stared at his reflection in the mirror—except it wasn't his. The face blinked a moment too late. A shadow moved behind his eyes.

Theo backed up a step. "This... this isn't science."

Thorne's hand trembled as he removed his glasses. "No. It's inheritance."

Valeska stepped closer to the pendulum. "You mean we were meant to find it?"

Kai didn't answer. He looked at her the way one looks at a puzzle that almost makes sense—until it doesn't.

"It found us."

Then the pendulum stopped.

Dead still.

The mirrored walls cracked—not shattered, just a single fracture across each surface, like veins of frozen lightning.

And then

Everything went silent.

No wind. No breath. Not even thought.

Just—

A name.

Spoken not aloud, but from within.

Each of them heard it. A name none had ever learned, yet all of them knew. A name that wasn't a word, but a return.

The floor beneath them pulsed once—like a heartbeat.

Then it ended.

OUTSIDE, LONDON BREATHED like it hadn't in centuries.

Aetherford's lower levels no longer existed. At least, not there. Where the basement had been was now just a wall—smooth, undisturbed stone, as though no door had ever been carved, no steps ever spiraled.

Kai stood in the courtyard, coat still dusted with old air, eyes on the skyline.

The city had changed.

Not visibly. But like someone had shifted one key on a piano. Everything still played—just wrong.

Theo was checking every brick of the sealed wall. "This isn't just a lock. It's a scar. Someone rewrote this place."

Valeska stared at the street beyond the university gates. "Feels like something's watching."

Kai spoke low. "It is."

Professor Thorne lit a cigarette with a shaking hand. "You said it wasn't a prophecy. That it was recall. That we never left. Then what was the dream?"

Kai's eyes narrowed as a black cab passed the gate slowly—too slowly.

He didn't answer Thorne. Instead, he whispered:

"Valeska. With me."

She was already moving.

Five Hours Later East London, beneath a disused viaduct

The wind howled like a ghost trapped in iron ribs. Beneath the arches, spray-painted sigils and burnt wax lay scattered like someone had tried—and failed—to erase something old.

Kai knelt over the soot.

His fingers hovered above the ashes, not touching. Reading.

"This was a veil ritual. Incomplete. Someone tried to open a path."

Valeska folded her arms. "A path to where?"

He glanced up. "Not where. When."

Her brow furrowed. "You think the dream, the body, the pendulum... it's all part of someone messing with time?"

Kai stood, brushing ash from his gloves. "No. This isn't about breaking time."

He looked into the shadows beyond the bridge. His voice dropped to that low, cutting calm.

"This is about unburying it."

Midnight Kai's flat—Holborn, London

Maps lay spread across the floor. Circles drawn around places that no longer appeared on satellite images. His walls were covered with dates. Incidents. Obituaries of people who shouldn't have died. Events that didn't make the news. A blood-red thread connected them all.

Theo stood in the doorway, stunned.

"You've been researching this for months."

Kai didn't turn. "Years."

"Why didn't you tell us?"

"Because it wasn't your story yet."

Theo stepped closer. "And now?"

Kai pulled a file from a hidden drawer. Yellowed paper. Police emblems. Case closed.

Except at the bottom:

Subject: Kai Starling

Status: Deceased

Date of Death: 17th August, 1981

Theo's voice cracked. "But... that's not possible."

Kai looked at him, eyes cold as mercury.

"That's what I thought too."

Theo stared at the paper like it might disappear. Like it should.

"You died before I was even born."

Kai didn't blink. "So did half the people on my wall."

Theo shook his head. "This is insane."

"No." Kai tapped the date. "This is a pattern."

He crossed the room, lifted a section of the floorboards, and drew out an old leather case. He placed it on the table and opened it. Inside: ancient photographs, ritual diagrams, a rusted locket with a faded symbol.

Theo frowned. "Where did you get all this?"

Kai didn't answer.

Instead, he lifted a photograph—grainy, black and white. It showed a group of six people standing in front of a building long since demolished. One of them looked exactly like Kai.

Exactly.

Same eyes. Same scar. Same impossible presence.

"1952," Kai said. "The year the dreams first came."

Theo's breath caught.

"They've been repeating this cycle every thirty years. Always different names. Same roles. Always ending in fire."

Theo moved to the window, heart racing. Outside, London slept beneath rain and silence. But something was watching. Something had followed them out of Aetherford.

Theo whispered, "Why thirty years?"

Kai's voice was distant, like echo off cathedral stone.

"Because that's how long it takes to forget."

1:08 A.M. Underground Archives – Clerkenwell District

The old vault had no official records. No electricity. Just dust and memory.

Kai moved alone now. Hood pulled up, footsteps silent.

He stopped before a steel door, rusted and painted over with warnings in dead languages.

He traced the mark again. The same sigil from the chalk wall beneath Aetherford.

He exhaled, placed his palm flat—and the door opened inward with a sound like falling teeth.

Inside, everything was cold.

Not the temperature. The feeling. Like he'd stepped into a memory that never wanted to be remembered.

He lit a lantern and stepped forward.

Stacks of files. Names crossed out. Witness reports shredded but never destroyed. Blood evidence. Journals signed with initials that matched the ones from the pendulum's whisper.

And on a table in the center: a box.

No lock.

Just a mirror embedded in the lid—cracked in the same vein pattern as the walls back at Aetherford.

Kai reached for it—

The mirror flickered.

Not his face.

But hers.

The girl with silver eyes.

She smiled.

"Kai," she whispered.

Then the mirror shattered.

And the pulse returned.

But this time, it spoke.

"Come home."

2:03 A.M.

The Abandoned Observatory – Southbank

It was once part of the old Royal Institute. Shut down in the '60s. Since then? Forgotten. Except by one.

Kai entered slow. No footsteps. Just breath.

A single chair waited beneath the shattered dome. A man sat in it, back straight. His shadow stretched long and crooked under the flickering light of a broken planetarium model.

Kai knew the face.

Not from memory.

From the mirror.

The girl with silver eyes had whispered his name. But this man?

He was the one who answered.

The man didn't turn around.

"You were never supposed to come this far," he said.

Kai's voice was ice. "You made it personal."

The man chuckled. "There is no personal. There's only pattern."

Kai circled him, slow, studying the floor. Chalk circles. Mirror shards. Blood not yet dry.

"You altered our dreams," Kai said. "Layered false memories over real ones. And when we got close, you planted the body."

The man smiled.

"But you still believed it, didn't you?"

Kai didn't answer.

Instead, he reached into his coat and tossed a file on the ground. Yellowed. Burnt at the edges.

The man's name was on it.

Professor Emeritus Rowan Mallgrave.

Deceased: 1979.

Cause: Suicide.

Theo's voice rang from the shadows, furious:

"We checked the records. You died!"

Rowan stood at last, eyes bright as firelight. "I did."

Kai's jaw tensed. "So who are you now?"

Rowan grinned.

"I'm what's left when time forgets to finish the story."

He stepped closer—one foot inside the chalk ring.

Valeska, from behind, whispered: "Don't let him speak the name."

Kai's eyes never left Rowan. "Already did."

Tick.

Tock.

The pendulum—though miles away—swung again.

Reality flickered.

Rowan wasn't real.

Or rather—he was... once. But now, he was a ghost with memory, not flesh. A remnant trapped in ritual. A man who killed himself to escape time, and instead, became part of it.

Kai whispered, "You didn't fake your death."

"You weaponised it."

Rowan tilted his head. "But I didn't kill anyone."

Kai smirked.

"No. You made us do it."

Theo gasped.

The dreams.

The symbols.

The anchor.

Rowan had manipulated their dreams into becoming reenactments. Like ancient plays with new actors. And someone among them... had snapped.

Valeska stepped forward.

Her hand was trembling.

"You mean the murder under Aetherford—"

Kai turned to her.

"Wasn't a murder."

He looked back at Rowan.

"It was a ritual sacrifice. To complete the cycle."

Rowan clapped, slow. "Bravo, Starling."

Then his face cracked—literally cracked—and a scream poured out like smoke.

The chalk ring ignited.

Kai didn't flinch.

"You made one mistake," he said.

Rowan's melting form turned. "Oh?"

"You thought we were still dreaming."

Kai held up the pendulum's core—no longer swinging. Just glowing. Sealed.

Rowan's eyes went wide.

"No..."

Kai smiled faintly.

"Dream's over."

He dropped the core into the fire.

The observatory shook. Mirrors shattered. Rowan screamed—not in pain, but in memory. Every lie he'd built burned with him.

And in that moment—

The pulse died.

4:00 A.M.

Back in Holborn

Theo sat with his head in his hands. Valeska was silent. Declan hadn't spoken in half an hour.

Kai stood at the window. Rain traced the glass.

"We stopped it," Theo said. "Right?"

Kai didn't answer.

He turned the page of a new file. One none of them had seen before. A missing person's report.

Filed yesterday.

A name circled in red.

Not Rowan.

Not a stranger.

But someone they all knew.

Valeska Monroe.

Kai's voice was barely a whisper.

"She was never here."

Chapter Three

The Echo Without a Voice

London, 3:47 AM

Smoke. Rain. Silence with a heartbeat.

The city whispered like an old ghost tonight.

Holborn's alleys were slick with memories—wet cobblestones that reflected nothing, as if light itself refused to remember this part of London.

Kai stood beneath a rusted fire escape, collar up, cigarette burning slow between his lips.

The rain didn't touch him. Not because of shelter—because it didn't dare.

Across the street, an unmarked door buzzed twice and opened a slit.

"Kai Starling," the voice rasped. "You're late."

Kai stepped forward, hand inside his coat—not for warmth, but for weight.

Cold steel. A 1937 Webley Mk IV revolver, loaded with KTW armor-piercing rounds. A whisper from a darker age.

"Time's never late," Kai muttered. "Just underestimated."

The man smirked. "Still quoting dead poets?"

Kai pushed past him.

Inside was another world.

Dark wood. Low lights. Smell of whiskey and regret.

And in the corner booth—Valeska, already two fingers deep into a bottle of Caol Ila 25. A flame in a storm.

She raised an eyebrow. "You brought a gun to a meeting?"

Kai sat. "I brought memory. The gun just came along."

She slid a manila envelope toward him. "Job's changed."

He didn't touch it.

"How bad?"

She didn't blink. "The kind that doesn't pay in money."

Kai leaned back, eyes scanning the bar.

"Who dies this time?"

Valeska poured another glass, but not for herself.

"For him," she said softly, lifting it in a silent toast.

Kai followed her eyes to the empty stool beside them.

"Declan?" he asked.

She nodded. "His sister called. Said he never made it home after the last train."

Kai's jaw tightened. He took the glass, clinked it against hers without a word, and drank.

A long silence.

"He always said," Valeska murmured, "that if he ever went missing, we shouldn't look for him. Just follow the music."

Kai looked at her sharply. "What music?"

She didn't answer. Instead, from outside the bar, the faintest sound rose—a violin. Just a few haunting notes. Echoes in the rain.

Kai was on his feet before the glass hit the table.

He stepped outside.

Rain still falling.

But there, beneath a broken streetlamp... a single black violin case.

No footprints. No figure. Just the music.

And under the case—

—a note.

Scrawled in Declan's handwriting:

"I remember now. Everything."

Kai knelt, brushing the rain off the paper.

A strange smile touched his lips. One not of joy. Not quite sorrow.

But something between. Like the edge of a dream that was never supposed to be real.

London, 4:02 AM

The rain had grown colder—sharper, as if the city had decided to weep in silence.

The knock came once. Firm. No urgency. No hesitation.

Valeska opened the door—gun in hand.

There stood Rehaan—coat soaked through, storm-grey eyes beneath a wide-brimmed hat. Untouched by time, but marked by years.

Kai stepped beside her, surprised only by how unsurprised he felt.

They stared—two ghosts from the same war, returned.

Rehaan smirked faintly. "Still breathing, then."

Kai nodded. "That depends who's asking."

Valeska lowered the pistol but didn't holster it. "You're late, Rehaan."

He raised an eyebrow. "You haven't changed."

Valeska scoffed. "You clearly have—if you're knocking instead of kicking doors."

Rehaan stepped in like he never left.

Same coat. Same silence. Same unfinished business.

Kai poured a glass. No offer was needed. Rehaan took it.

Then he pulled a photograph from his coat and laid it on the table.

A man. Dead. Chicago alley.

Gunshot to the chest.

A silver bullet casing beside him.

But it wasn't the corpse that mattered.

It was the word scrawled behind him in red:

"KAI STARLING"

Valeska's breath hitched. Kai's glass didn't tremble—but his fingers did.

Rehaan looked them both in the eye.

"They're back. And they're digging. Every secret we buried—they're unearthing it piece by piece."

Kai picked up the photo, stared at it.

Then, without looking up, he said:

"Then it's time to remind them—I never died."

REHAAN SAT DOWN, JAW tight, eyes fixed on the photo.

But he wasn't looking at the body anymore. He was reading between the bloodstains.

"You gonna tell me," he muttered, "how the hell Valeska got back into this?"

Kai leaned against the table, lit another cigarette. This time, it shook just a little.

"She found me," he said.

Valeska didn't deny it. She just lit her own and stared at the window like it might answer for her.

Kai continued, voice low—measured, like recounting a memory too real to dream:

"Last month. I was in a detox clinic in Blackheath—under another name, trying to forget one too many truths. That's where she walked in. No warning. No explanation. Just said, 'They're watching again, and I don't want to die without knowing why.'"

Rehaan narrowed his eyes. "And you believed her?"

Kai didn't blink.

"I never stopped."

Valeska looked at him then. Not softly. But like a mirror might—reflecting the exact damage he refused to admit.

Rehaan leaned back. "So she finds you, drops a mystery, and you both jump back into the fire?"

Kai exhaled smoke and nodded once.

"This isn't just another case. It's everything we left undone. It's all the files we buried, the names we burned, the nights we don't talk about."

He glanced at the manila envelope.

"Declan died chasing shadows we swore didn't exist anymore."

Rehaan's voice darkened. "And the title of this little opera we're dancing in again?"

Kai's smile was faint. But bitter.

"Material. Drugs. Dreams. That's what it's always been."

Valeska spoke for the first time in minutes.

"We chased the material—files, weapons, blood-money, artefacts no one should've touched. We ran with the drugs—hallucinogens, nootropics, memory enhancers, the shit that makes you see things not from this world. And the dreams..."

She stopped.

Kai picked up where she left off.

"...were what it all led to. Warnings. Messages. Codes. Nightmares we couldn't wake up from."

Rehaan's jaw clenched. "So we're not chasing a killer."

Kai shook his head.

"No. We're chasing a design. A system older than us. And someone is rewriting it."

A gust of wind knocked against the window.

Valeska whispered:

"She was never here."

Rehaan frowned. "Who?"

Kai looked down at the photograph again.

Then up at the wall—at all the obituaries, the maps, the names.

His voice was colder now. Focused.

"Whoever's behind this—they've erased people from memory. From history. And they're starting to erase us too."

A long silence.

Rehaan picked up his coat. "Then we better start remembering fast."

Kai nodded. "Because the last time we forgot... people died."

The room went quiet again. Not dead—but listening.

Outside, thunder rolled like memory cracking open.

And somewhere, in a place none of them could name, a second name was being erased.

They didn't know it yet.

But the clock had already started.

London, 5:12 AM

A cold mist had crept in through the window cracks, curling around Kai's boots like fog remembering old footsteps. Rehaan stood near the bulletin board, eyes flicking over the tangle of red string, pins, and newsprint headlines—each one a lie told just convincingly enough to be archived.

Valeska sat on the armrest of the couch, silent, her cigarette burning down to ash between her fingers.

"Tell me about the girl," Rehaan said finally. "The violin. The case. The note."

Kai took a breath, slow and sharp.

"That was Declan's last breadcrumb."

He crossed to the table and pulled open a drawer, tossing down a folder labeled: VERITY PROGRAM.

Inside: grainy surveillance stills, torn letters, and chemical schematics written in ciphered German.

Valeska stood. "It's not just about us anymore. Whatever we were chasing back then—they've weaponized it. The dreams... they're not dreams now. They're triggers."

Rehaan's brow furrowed. "Triggers for what?"

Kai looked at him.

"Memories that don't belong to you."

A long pause.

Rehaan cracked his knuckles. "Then we're up against something that doesn't just kill bodies."

Kai: "It rewrites souls."

A crack split the air.

Not thunder.

Gunfire.

A sharp, historic bark—Webley Mk VI, .455 calibre, the kind issued in 1915 and never quite forgotten by those who knew how to hold it. A gentleman's sidearm. A war dog's whisper. And now—Kai's second heartbeat.

The window behind them shattered. Rehaan ducked.

Kai didn't.

He stood.

And fired back.

One shot.

Clean. Centered. Through the dark.

Somewhere out there, a man fell without a name. Another name gone.

Valeska was already moving, flipping the table, dragging a second revolver from her thigh holster. Her voice was calm—ice in a hurricane.

"They're here faster than expected."

Rehaan crawled to cover, teeth clenched. "They?"

Kai exhaled. "Archivists."

"The ones from Berlin?"

"No." Valeska reloaded. "The ones we buried under it."

Rain poured in through the broken window. The bar lights flickered.

A violin cried somewhere in the fog.

The smoke cleared just enough to see the silhouette outside—slumped against a wrought iron post, gun still warm in his hand. One of theirs. Or one of someone's.

Kai stepped over the glass, straightened his coat. The Webley dangled casually from two fingers like a reminder—he didn't raise it unless he meant to end something.

Rehaan stood, heart still catching up.

"You didn't flinch," he muttered.

Kai lit a match against his boot, brought the flame to the edge of his cigarette with the same ease a man might read poetry before bed.

"A gentleman doesn't flinch," Kai said. "Not when history's knocking."

Valeska raised an eyebrow. "We talking history now?"

Kai looked out into the London night—rain slicing the lamplight, puddles rippling like they remembered something they weren't supposed to.

"I grew up on Grafton Street," he said. "Where men wore suits even to lie. My father used to say, 'Never raise your voice, son. Raise your aim.'"

Rehaan gave a dry chuckle. "Did he also teach you to quote like a bleeding novel?"

Kai turned, eyes calm but ironclad. "No. That came after the funeral."

He tucked the Webley into his coat with surgical precision, then adjusted his cufflinks—silver, engraved. The letters K.S.E. shimmered beneath the barlight.

Valeska smirked. "Still wearing the Earl initials?"

Kai smiled faintly. "I earned the 'Earl' in the alleyways, not the ballroom. And titles only matter when blood's involved."

He pulled out a monogrammed handkerchief—white, silk, absurdly out of place—and wiped a speck of someone else's blood from his cheek.

Then he offered it to Rehaan.

"Clean up, would you? We're still in London. And some of us have reputations to keep."

Rehaan stared at him. Then took the cloth.

"Jesus Christ."

Kai tipped his head. "Close. But better dressed."

Across the Thames, far from the smoke and silence of Holborn, the night wore a different face—marble floors, obsidian windows, and a piano playing itself in a penthouse that looked down on the sleeping city like a god who no longer cared.

Geltorn Brith Earl stood barefoot, shirt unbuttoned, tie loose like a noose he'd learned to enjoy. A half-empty bottle of GlenDronach 1972 glowed amber on the table beside him—untouched. He never drank when he was planning.

And tonight, he was planning war.

Three screens flickered in front of him. Security feeds, satellite overlays, archived footage scrubbed from public record. But his eyes weren't on the images.

They were on the chessboard in front of him.

An ivory king sat alone, surrounded by pawns. Knights already fallen. Rooks abandoned. Only the queen was missing—absent, not dead. The most dangerous kind.

Geltorn moved the king forward one square. Smiled.

"Checkmate isn't about force," he murmured. "It's about forgetting where the first move was made."

He picked up a file—black leather, stitched at the edge. No name. Just a symbol burned into the front: a snake swallowing its own tail.

Inside—photos of Kai Starling, Rehaan, Valeska. Declan's death report. A map of Aetherford University circled in red.

And one more sheet. Blank. Waiting.

Geltorn dipped a fountain pen, wrote a name.

Only one word:

Kai.

Then he folded the file shut and whispered, as if to the glass itself:

"The dreamers are remembering."

He turned back to the city.

And smiled like a man who had never needed a god to make him dangerous.

Camden Market – 4:26 AM

Rain-slick rooftops. Neon signs flickering like dying stars. And somewhere between the rusted stairwells and broken clocks—violence, waiting to be heard.

Kai stepped into the alley like he'd been summoned there.

Trench coat dragging water, revolver holstered beneath. Not hidden—just resting, like a beast that only wakes when it tastes fear.

Behind him, Valeska adjusted her gloves. One finger at a time. Calm. Precise. The kind of calm that came from holding a scalpel to someone's memory and smiling while you cut.

Rehaan lit a match on a brick wall, used it to light a cigarette, then threw it into a puddle.

"Place reeks of setup."

Kai nodded. "That's why we showed up early."

Just then—

Crack.

Gunshot.

A slug tore through the air, embedding into the brick three inches from Rehaan's head. He didn't flinch.

"Winchester 1887," he muttered. "Modified choke. Close-range. Bastard's hunting."

Valeska crouched low, pulled out a M1911 from her thigh holster—polished chrome, ivory grip. "Only hunters miss the first shot. Snipers don't."

Kai drew his weapon—a Webley Mk VI, the revolver of old wars and older grudges.

He kissed the barrel, whispered, "Wake up."

Then they moved.

THE ALLEY TURNED INTO a storm of boots, bullets, and blood.

Rehaan flipped a trash bin, took cover, returned fire. "Two on the left, above the florist shop. Using elevation but no silencers. Amateurs."

Valeska vanished into smoke—only to reappear behind one of the shooters and knock him out cold with the butt of her pistol.

Kai walked forward like time was breaking for him.

He raised his Webley.

BOOM.

One shot. One man fell from the roof like a forgotten name.

Another figure stepped out of the shadow—full tactical gear, but no insignia. No face. Just a voice through static:

"You were warned to stay forgotten."

Kai raised his revolver again. "I don't listen well. Especially to ghosts."

BOOM.

The man dropped.

Silence returned. But it wasn't over.

Valeska stepped over a body and looked at Kai. "Why now?"

Kai reloaded. "Because someone's scared. They just told us what they're protecting."

Rehaan picked up a strange coin from one of the attackers. Not British. Not modern.

He turned it in the light.

"It's starting, isn't it?"

Kai lit a cigarette off the barrel of his gun.

"No, mate. It never ended. We just woke up again."

St. Elora's Chapel – Holloway – 6:03 AM

They said the church was decommissioned in '78.

But candles still burned inside.

And not the kind you light for salvation.

The rain had turned to mist. The air thick with incense and rusted hymns. Kai stepped through the arched oak doors like a man walking into a confession he already knew he'd regret.

Valeska followed, eyes sweeping every pew. Her heels echoed against stone like a ticking clock.

Rehaan stayed by the gate, watching shadows that moved too deliberately to be wind.

Inside—rows of robed women bowed in silence.

Nuns.

Or so they claimed.

Kai removed his hat and whispered, almost politely,

"Romans 16:17. 'Mark them which cause divisions and offences contrary to the doctrine which ye have learned; and avoid them.'"

One of the "nuns" looked up, too quickly.

Her smile was tight. Wrong. "We preach unity, not division, Mr. Starling."

Kai's smile was colder than marble.

"Then why do I smell cordite and chloroform instead of prayer and lavender?"

Another nun stepped forward. Younger. Blonde. A tattoo of a snake just visible above her collar.

"We serve God."

Kai stepped closer. "Then tell me why your altar's two degrees off true north. Why your crucifix lacks the INRI inscription. Why the stained-glass depicts St. Catherine holding Lucifer's lantern."

He turned to Rehaan. "This isn't a sanctuary. It's a façade."

Rehaan cracked his knuckles. "Say the word."

Valeska's eyes were already on the golden box behind the altar—just slightly open. "They're hiding something. Something old."

Suddenly, one of the nuns drew a pistol—from beneath her robes.

Kai moved like thunder split into flesh.

CRACK.

His Webley spat fire. The nun dropped—alive, but bleeding. Another reached for something at the altar—

But Valeska was faster.

She leapt, kicked the altar sideways, and grabbed the golden box mid-air before it could smash.

Rehaan had three more fake sisters on their knees in under five seconds.

Silence.

Kai opened the box.

Inside: pages. Ancient. Faded Latin and ink mixed with what looked like dried blood.

And something wrapped in silk.

He unwrapped it—slowly.

A rosary.

But each bead was carved from human tooth.

Rehaan looked disgusted. "That's not faith. That's a curse."

Kai ran his thumb across the crucifix.

Etched behind it, barely visible: Project G.O.S.P.E.L.

Underneath: "God. Operation. Synthetic. Psyche. Eternal. Light."

Valeska muttered, "They were testing religion like a drug..."

Kai closed the box.

"No. They were weaponizing belief. And this church isn't the first."

He turned to the "nuns," eyes like storm glass.

"You've been preaching dreams... but selling nightmares."

Undercroft – Beneath St. Elora's Chapel – 6:47 AM

The stairs were narrow. Cracked stone. Slick with damp. Carved centuries ago, before London had gaslights, before maps drew borders between myth and truth.

Kai ran his hand along the wall.

"These weren't built for the living," he said.

Rehaan grunted, "Then why are the dead carrying guns?"

Valeska led now. One hand on the pistol, the other brushing a faint engraving—worn by time, but still readable:

"Anno Domini 1666 – The Night the Sky Burned Red."

Kai read it aloud.

"Great Fire of London," he muttered. "But this place was here before that."

Valeska turned. "You're thinking what I'm thinking?"

Kai nodded. "Someone tried to burn the city to hide something."

They reached the bottom.

A heavy iron door. Marked not with a cross—but with a circle and triangle interlocked.

Rehaan stared. "What is that?"

Kai whispered:

"The Seal of the Forgotten Archive."

He kicked the door open.

Inside: a vault of chaos.

Ancient relics. Stacks of folders sealed in wax. Walls covered in maps, symbols, dates—threads pinned with twine connecting names long erased from history.

Valeska froze.

"1943. London. MI-26."

She pointed to a photograph—black and white—of soldiers around a machine that looked like a cross between a radio and a coffin.

Caption read: "Lucidity Field Test – Operation Candlelight – 4 Nov 1943 – Failed. Subject lost in dreamstate."

Kai grabbed another.

"June 2nd, 1972. Chicago. Subject #44 escaped containment. Witnesses describe 'phantom bleeding'—blood appearing without wounds."

He turned to Rehaan.

"You remember Geltorn's father disappeared that year?"

Rehaan nodded slowly. "You're telling me he was part of this?"

Valeska found another box—labeled "R.D.D Protocol"

Inside: drug vials. Vials marked with serial codes and handwritten notes.

R.D.D. – Recall. Dream. Death.

"1961—Berlin. Subject 003 survived six deaths. All in dreams. All real enough to leave scars."

Kai clenched his jaw. "This is why they created 'Project GOSPEL'. Religion, memory, pharmacology—all blurred. They weren't looking for God. They were building one."

Rehaan laughed, dark and short. "And calling it therapy."

Valeska picked up one last item.

A bullet. Blackened. With a cross carved into its casing.

Inscribed on the bottom: "Blessed in blood, 1815. Waterloo. Fired once. Hit twice."

She stared at Kai. "How does a bullet hit twice?"

Kai's voice dropped.

"When it returns."

The air began to shift. A low hum, electric and old.

The vault... was waking up.

Kai grabbed the folders.

"We take what we can. Burn the rest."

Rehaan stared at the glowing machine in the corner.

"What about that?"

Kai checked his watch.

"If it turns on by itself...

We don't wait to ask questions."

St. Elora's Chapel – Aboveground – Stormlight, 7:04 AM

Lightning cracked like a snapped neck.

They came out of the undercroft sweating, dust-covered, carrying folders that should never see daylight.

Kai wiped his hand on his coat—not because it was dirty, but because it trembled.

A group of sisters stood at the altar, heads bowed. Their lips moved, but no sound came.

Rehaan whispered, "They weren't here when we went down."

Valeska touched her pistol. "And they're not sisters."

Kai stepped forward, his voice soft but cutting through the silence like a scalpel.

"'Beware false prophets, which come to you in sheep's clothing, but inwardly they are ravening wolves.'"

His eyes scanned them.

"Matthew 7:15. You skipped that verse in Sunday Mass, didn't you?"

One of the "sisters" raised her head. The smile she wore was a fracture, not kindness.

"The Book won't save you, Starling," she said.

Kai's voice didn't flinch.

"It already did. Just not from what you think."

Flashback: Germany – Wewelsburg Castle – 1944

The page Kai pulled from the Archive showed grainy photos. A circle of high-ranking Nazi officers, standing around a map of Europe covered in red chalk.

"Traumkrieg."

The Dream War.

Below it, hand-scribbled in English:

"Not a battle of bullets. But memory. Erase the resistance, and you erase the rebellion."

A note attached:

"Subject Omega: Survived 7 dream assassinations. Exhibits advanced recall of parallel timelines. Test discontinued due to mental rupture."

◈

Back in the Chapel – Present

Rehaan opened a case:

Two guns, side-by-side.

Webley Mk VI revolver – 1915.

Customized SIG P210 – Zurich model. Serial scratched out.

He passed one to Kai.

"You ever use one of these?"

Kai checked the weight. Loaded. Smelled like prayers and rust.

"Only in dreams," he muttered.

The "sisters" started moving.

Their eyes flickered—not light, but memory itself shifting, rewriting.

One raised her sleeve. A tattoo. Not ink—numbers burned into skin.

A number from Auschwitz.

Below it:

R.D.D. Test Subject 12.

Codename: Miriam.

Kai stepped forward. "They weren't just testing drugs. They were testing belief. Injecting fear. Forcing people to dream the same thing... until it became real."

Valeska gasped.

"They turned faith into a weapon."

Thunder again. But this time, inside the walls.

Something ancient stirred. The stained-glass windows cracked—light bleeding in strange shapes.

A voice echoed—but it spoke inside their heads.

"You shouldn't have remembered."

Outside – Black Car Watching From the Fog

Geltorn Brith Earl lit a cigar. His gloved hands didn't shake.

A man behind him whispered, "They've entered the threshold."

Geltorn didn't blink.

"Good," he said. "Let them remember. Let them piece it together. But when they reach the final door..."

He flicked the ash out the window.

"Make sure it opens from the outside only."

Psychological file recovered from Archive:

Date: 17 July 1977

Subject: Declan Veer

Entry 44 – Final

"They told me dreams aren't real. Then why can I still hear the screams every time I close my eyes? I saw it. I saw London break in two—once in 1871, once in 1993. And we haven't even reached the second time yet."

When Memory Turns to Smoke

London, 4:12 AM.

Rain whispered secrets through the cracked stone of St. Augustine's—an abandoned church on the edge of Holloway. Candlelight flickered in stained glass windows long forgotten by time, casting fractured saints across the pews.

Kai Starling stepped in, boots echoing like a clock ticking backwards. The cold met him like an old friend—familiar, unwelcome, and truthful.

The altar had been stripped years ago. But someone had lit six candles in a perfect crescent. A violin case rested at the center. Not black this time—wooden. Carved. As if made by hands that remembered every hymn ever sung here.

"Rehaan," Kai called softly. "You feel that?"

Rehaan nodded. "This place breathes like it never died."

Valeska stepped forward, her coat soaked, curls clinging to her face. "This isn't just a meeting place. It's a reenactment."

Kai's eyes scanned the rafters. "Last time I was in this church, I was nine. My father was shot outside that very door. A Webley Mk VI. 455 calibre. 1915 make. He bled onto the stone and whispered scripture."

He walked to the candle circle.

"John 8:32," he murmured.

"'And ye shall know the truth, and the truth shall make you free.'"

From the shadows, a voice hissed: "Unless truth kills you first."

Three figures stepped out. Robed. Faces hidden by veils like nuns—but something was wrong. Their steps were too calculated. Too silent.

Rehaan's hand went to his coat. Valeska already had hers on the grip of a Beretta 93R—custom silencer, vintage navy issue.

Kai didn't flinch. "Fake Sisters of Mercy. Seen them before. East Berlin, 1986. Operated under Vatican documents that never existed. Used psilocybin-laced communion wafers to erase memory from defectors."

He stepped closer, voice colder now. "Who sent you?"

One raised her hand. Slowly. Her fingers glowed red—tiny circuit tattoos pulsing with low voltage.

Valeska drew. "Back up. Now."

The nun smiled. Too wide. Too calm.

"This place holds a file," she said. "One sealed under the floorboard in 1953. Signed by Alan Turing. We came to burn it."

Kai's eyes lit with fire. "You're not burning history."

The first shot came from the bell tower. A Remington 700 sniper round. Clean. Silent.

But it missed.

Kai dove. Rolled behind the pew. Drew his revolver—an Enfield No. 2 Mk I, 1932. The shot echoed like a hymn.

One nun dropped.

The other two fled into the vestry.

Valeska kicked open the rear door. Rehaan followed.

Kai remained. Eyes on the violin case. On the candlelight. On the past.

He picked it up and opened it slowly.

Inside wasn't a violin.

It was a tape recorder.

Marked:

"Play only when London forgets."

He pressed play.

A voice. Old. Female.

"I was Sister Madeline. And I remember. Everything. The dreams weren't dreams. They were trials. Codes. Designed to warn us about the ones rewriting our minds..."

Kai's hand trembled.

Outside, the church bells rang once.

And far across the Thames, a fire bloomed in an archive that should've never existed.

LOCATION: THAMESIDE Classified Archives, Deptford, London

Time: 4:41 AM

Date: 6 April 2025 — exactly 72 years after the file was first sealed on 6 April 1953, hours after the death of Alan Turing's confidant, Dr. Elias Ward.

The flames ate the building slow and deliberate, as if history itself were choking on its own secrets. But it wasn't just the fire—no. It was precision. Silent charges. Thermite in the ventilation. Files didn't burn; they vanished.

And in a black 1991 Jaguar XJR parked across the street, a man watched. He wore gloves stitched from Czech leather, sunglasses tinted blue, and a wristwatch set precisely eight minutes ahead.

Geltorn Brith Earl.

Handsome. Composed. A face for Vanity Fair but eyes trained like an old soldier. He watched the inferno not with awe, but calculation.

Behind him, in the passenger seat, sat a child—barely twelve. Blindfolded. Humming a hymn that hadn't been sung since the Coventry Ritual of 1810.

Geltorn leaned forward, adjusting the rearview mirror.

"They're waking up," he said. "And they're remembering too fast."

He dialled a number.

A voice on the other end, thick German accent: "Status?"

"Stage One complete. Archives gone. But Starling retrieved the audio."

Silence. Then: "And the child?"

"Still singing."

"Take her to Whitby. Sea remembers what land buries."

Click.

Geltorn tossed the phone onto the seat and turned to the girl.

"You're not afraid, are you?"

The child smiled faintly. "They buried her name, but she still prays."

Geltorn paused. That voice—it wasn't hers. It wasn't... now.

He started the engine. The rain picked up like something wanted to wash the city clean.

Back in Holloway, Kai stared at the old recorder, its tape spinning slowly, rewinding.

Valeska stepped beside him, her voice tight. "The nun's body is gone."

Kai didn't flinch. "They dissolve after five minutes. Bioengineered for silence. Developed in Vienna, 1979. A program called MERCY.EXE."

Rehaan returned, breathing hard. "The others vanished into smoke. No trace. But..."

He held up a photograph.

It showed Geltorn Brith Earl.

Standing beside a government official in 1993.

And beside them?

Theo Grimsley.

But the date on the back said 1985—when Theo would've been barely a child.

Kai whispered, "This isn't just about time. It's about memory that loops. Folds. Rewrites."

Valeska looked at the sky through a broken pane of glass.

"Then we're already late."

Kai loaded a fresh round into his revolver.

"Not if we find the next point."

Rehaan raised an eyebrow. "Where?"

Kai turned. His voice low. Final.

"Chicago. 1995. The dream begins there."

London, 4:57 AM.

Kai stood still beneath the spitting rain, smoke from his cigarette curling upward into the wet night air. His thoughts scattered like loose pages in the wind, but in the quiet of the aftermath, one truth remained sharp, undeniable.

He leaned back, imagining the thrilling possibilities that lay ahead, knowing that the best cases—and perhaps the best connections—were still waiting to unfold.

And as he lit one last cigarette beneath the waking London sky, he whispered to no one and everyone:

"You know, if mystery were a drink... I'd order a double shot of you."

9 789334 278026

Printed at Repro India Ltd.